R
O

Dinosaur Hunter

Steve Barlow and Steve Skidmore

Illustrated by Judit Tondora

Franklin Watts
First published in Great Britain in 2019 by The Watts Publishing Group

Text © Steve Barlow and Steve Skidmore 2019
Illustrations by Judit Tondora © Franklin Watts 2019
The "2Steves" illustration by Paul Davidson
used by kind permission of Orchard Books

PB ISBN 978 1 4451 6963 7
ebook ISBN 978 1 4451 6964 4
Library ebook ISBN 978 1 4451 6965 1

1 3 5 7 9 10 8 6 4 2

Printed in Great Britain

MIX
Paper from
responsible sources
FSC® C104740

Franklin Watts
An imprint of
Hachette Children's Group
Part of The Watts Publishing Group
Carmelite House
50 Victoria Embankment
London EC4Y 0DZ

An Hachette UK Company
www.hachette.co.uk

www.franklinwatts.co.uk

How to be a hero

This book is not like others you have read. This is a choose-your-own-destiny book where YOU are the hero of this adventure.

Each section of this book is numbered. At the end of most sections, you will have to make a choice. Each choice will take you to a different section of the book.

If you choose correctly, you will succeed. But be careful. If you make a bad choice, you may have to start the adventure again. If this happens, make sure you learn from your mistake!

Go to the next page to start your adventure. And remember, don't be a zero, be a hero!

You are an animal tracker, famous for photographing and filming big game. Your expertise means you are often called on to dart endangered animals with sedatives so that they can be studied by scientists and veterinary surgeons or moved to a safer place away from poachers and hunters.

After a long day tracking a jaguar that has been living a little too close to villagers in Guatemala, you have succeeded in finding the big cat at last. You are just about to dart the animal so he can be moved to a safer environment in a more remote area ... when your satellite phone goes off.

Go to 1.

1

"This is General Sanchez of the Mexican Army Special Forces," squawks the phone. "We have an emergency. A new cenote has appeared in Yucatán province."

You know that a cenote is a deep, water-filled sinkhole, created when the roof of an underground cavern collapses.

"I'm sorry, General," you say. "I don't see how I can help."

"Dinosaurs have emerged from the cenote. It seems they have been trapped in the caverns below it for millions of years. They are coming out. Now will you help us?"

To refuse to help, go to 14.
To agree to help, go to 22.

2

It is dark as you set off in the jeep, using GPS to find your way to the cenote.

The forest roads are dirt track, muddy and rutted. Progress is slow.

You turn a bend in the road. In your headlights, you see movement in the trees ahead.

To try to creep past whatever is causing it, go to 21.

To use the jeep's searchlight to see what it is, go to 13.

3

You raise the dart gun and fire at the bodies you can see in the torchlight. You bring two down. But a third picks up the torch in its powerful claws, crushing it.

Now you cannot see; but you can hear that the rest of the deadly predators are closing in on you.

There is only one escape.

Go to 27.

4

You spot a small cave mouth and head for it. But the velociraptors race in pursuit, and they are much faster than you are.

When you feel their breath on the back of your neck, you know there is only one way out.

Go to 27.

5

At first light, you find your way onto a forest road that is crammed with fleeing villagers. They tell you they have been terrorised by a giant reptile.

From their descriptions, it sounds like a Tyrannosaurus rex.

To track down the T. rex alone, go to 43.

To use the radio to call for support, go to 49.

When you arrive at the gate, the priest is looking up into the angry sky. He is chanting with outstretched arms. To your astonishment, the storm clouds break up and disappear.

The old man turns to you. "My people are in danger," he says. "You have come to help them, so I will help you." He hands you a medallion, decorated with a feathered serpent. "This amulet is sacred to our ancestors. If you are in deadly danger, call for help and their spirits will return you to this time and place."

You seriously doubt this but you take the medallion and thank the priest.

It is late afternoon when you return to the briefing room. "We need an aerial survey of the cenote," you say.

"Yes," says Duarte, "but is it too late to start today?"

To set off at once, go to 19.
To wait until the next day, go to 42.

7

You decide to take cover in the wreck and wait for daylight.

Hearing a rustle in the bushes all around you, you light a hand-flare to drive off any predators. But the flare sets fire to spilled fuel from the jeep, which instantly becomes an inferno. You are driven back, weapon-less, into the forest — which is suddenly full of hungry reptilian eyes. You have only one chance of survival.

Go to 27.

8

You seize one of the vines trailing from the collapsed roof, and swing across to the island.

The dinosaurs are reluctant to take to the water to follow you, but you cannot stay where you are. The countdown you have set on the charges has begun. Time is short!

To try to climb to the surface, go to 23.
To call up the helicopter, go to 25.

9

You run up one side of the pyramid-shaped ruin, hoping to find shelter in the small temple on the top.

But the many steps are hard to climb, and the velociraptors spot you. They climb the steps easily. Soon they are closing in on every side. There is no escape.

Go to 27.

10

You surface and reach for the rope by which you came down.

But with all the weight of the diving gear, you cannot climb quickly. You look down and see the monster rising from the depths, jaws gaping to engulf you.

Go to 27.

11

You snatch a flare pistol from the emergency pack and fire.

The flare explodes in the pterosaur's face. It flies away, screeching with alarm. You guess it has been underground so long that it can no longer stand bright light.

As the helicopter flies again over the cenote, you point down at a ramp made of earth and shattered rock leading from deep inside the earth to the rim of the hole.

"That's how the dinosaurs are getting out," you say. "If we can destroy that ramp, they'll be trapped again. But we'll need explosive charges, and I can't see anywhere the helicopter can land."

The Sun is setting as you return to the army base.

To wait for daylight to act further, go to 42.

To return at once to the cenote, go to 31.

"I need bolt cutters!" you cry.

The winch-man drops you a pair. Hanging upside down, you cut through the ropes holding the rest of the ladder beneath you.

The ropes snap apart. The T. rex falls back and the helicopter lifts away. It has just cleared the lip of the cavern when the charges go off. A vast cloud of dust and debris bursts from the hole. When it clears, you see that the ramp has collapsed. The dinosaurs are once again trapped in their underground lair!

Go to 50.

13

The bright beam of the searchlight reveals a heavily armoured dinosaur with a clubbed tail — an ankylosaurus. It is not happy about being disturbed! It gives an angry roar and charges the jeep.

You try to drive away, but the jeep's wheels spin uselessly. It is stuck in the mud!

To get out of the jeep and run, go to 36.

To try to free the jeep, go to 29.

14

"Either this is a joke," you say, "or you're crazy."

The voice on the phone becomes angry. "If you won't help, we'll find someone else. Your hunting permit for Mexico is revoked."

The call cuts off. You realise you have made a mistake. You were due to film a major wildlife series in Mexico next month.

Several hours later, as you head for the local airport, your phone rings again. "We still need your help, Señor." General Sanchez sounds desperate.

"I thought you were finding someone else," you say.

"We did. He didn't work out."

"You mean a dinosaur got him?"

"*Si.*"

You gulp. That sounds bad. But nobody ever said hunting dinosaurs would be a walk in the park.

Go to 22.

15

Dropping your equipment, you run for your life.

It's no good. The velociraptors are more powerful than you, and much, much faster, and now you don't even have a torch!

As the pack closes in, you take your last chance to survive.

Go to 27.

16

You wade into the swamp. The mud gives off a strong smell of rotting plants, masking your scent. You are under cover by the time the velociraptors appear. But you have been lucky so far. You will need a plan to deal with them.

As you emerge from the swamp, you find a large animal trail. You risk lighting a match, and find the tracks of a large dinosaur, probably a triceratops. The tracks give you an idea.

To steer clear of the tracks, go to 35.
To follow the tracks, go to 28.

17

"We can't risk waiting," you say. "The weather could change. Let's just trap as many dinosaurs as we can."

You head for the cenote, unslinging your backpack of high explosive charges. A roar brings you to a halt. You look up to find that the Tyrannosaurus rex has been hiding and guarding the head of the ramp, possibly looking for easy prey.

And it's just found you!

Go to 27.

18

The moment you enter the water, you are mobbed by clidastes — crocodile-like marine reptiles. They are ferocious and, at four metres long, too big for you to handle.

There is only one escape.

Go to 27.

19

You order the helicopter to be prepared for take-off.

Soon, you are flying above the dense forest of the Yucatán. The cenote is a dark hole far below and you can see dinosaurs moving among the trees.

Hearing a terrible screech, you look up. A huge flying dinosaur, a pterosaur, is diving towards the helicopter.

To try to escape the pterosaur, go to 46.
To shoot it with your dart gun, go to 37.

You use the drones to watch as the dinosaurs head down the ramp.

Duarte points at the drone operator's screen. "The T. rex seems to be guarding the top of the ramp. Can we drive it away?"

You shake your head. "And sunlight doesn't seem to bother it. We need to find another way in."

You explain to Duarte that many cenotes are connected by underground rivers. "If we can find another one, I'll use the scuba gear to reach the dinosaurs' cavern."

The drones locate another cenote nearby. You get suited up in diving gear and abseil down into the deep hole.

On reaching the water, you dive to look for a passage into the dinosaurs' cavern, only to find yourself face-to-face with a gigantic marine reptile — a liopleurodon.

To swim for the surface and escape, go to 10.

To dive deeper and escape, go to 32.

You turn off the headlights and creep past the disturbance.

Moments later, there is a splash and the jeep starts to sink. In the darkness, you have driven into a swamp.

You rev the engine to try and reverse out. The noise attracts a heavily armoured dinosaur — an ankylosaurus.

The creature roars with anger and starts to pound the jeep to smithereens with its powerful, clubbed tail. You realise that you have come to the end of the road.

Go to 27.

22

"All right," you say, "I'll help."

You are flown to Yucatán by a Mexican military helicopter. The sky is dark with storm clouds as you land at an army base.

An officer steps forwards and salutes. "I'm Captain Duarte. General Sanchez has ordered me to see that you have all you need."

In the briefing room, you examine maps showing the positions of the cenote and dinosaur sightings.

"Our scientists," says Duarte, "think these creatures were trapped in the caverns when the K-T meteorite strike killed all the other dinosaurs, sixty-six million years ago."

You give Duarte a list of equipment you will need. She frowns. "Drones? Scuba gear? What do you need those for?"

Before you can reply, a corporal appears at the door. "Sir, there's a Mayan priest at the gate. He says he must speak to you."

To agree to speak to the priest, go to 6.
To refuse, go to 34.

23

You try to climb using vines and tree roots. Both are slippery, and your progress is slow. You are only halfway to safety when the charges start to go off. You have just one hope for survival.

Go to 27.

24

You switch on an electric torch and make your way through the forest, using animal trails to guide your way as you hack through dense undergrowth.

Hearing a noise behind you, you drop the torch and hide. Peering through the leaves, you see several wicked-looking dinosaurs gathering around the light — velociraptors!

To use the radio to call for help, go to 47.

To run, go to 15.

To use the dart gun, go to 3.

25

You grab your radio. "I need the helicopter!"

"I'm sending it in now," crackles Duarte's voice.

The helicopter appears, descending through the hole in the roof and firing flares to drive off the pterosaurs. A steel ladder dangles beneath it. You grab it and start to climb. But the T. rex lunges across the lake and grasps the last rung of the ladder in its mighty jaws!

To call for a gun, go to 44.
To call for a flare, go to 39.
To call for bolt cutters, go to 12.

26

You slip away without a sound. Smelling a sweet perfume, you belly-crawl into a grove of frangipani trees, hoping that their scent will mask yours. It works! From your hiding place, you watch the velociraptors go by.

You crawl out of hiding and keep moving until you emerge into a small clearing. In front of you stands a ruined Mayan temple. To your left is a swamp, to your right stands some tall trees.

But a crashing noise from behind you tells you that the velociraptors have picked up your scent again.

To hide in the temple, go to 9.
To climb a tree, go to 38.
To wade into the swamp, go to 16.

27

You grasp the medallion. "Spirits of the Maya, help me!"

There is a burst of light and a mighty, rushing wind. You find yourself back at the gate of the army camp.

The old Mayan priest looks at you sorrowfully. "You cannot help my people if you perish. You must choose more carefully next time."

You thank the priest and head for the helicopter. You have a job to do...

Go to 19.

28

You follow the trail, being deliberately noisy to attract the velociraptors.

Hearing a noise behind, you turn to see the pack on your heels. You speed up, and almost run full-tilt into a grazing triceratops.

You dodge past the startled dinosaur, but the velociraptors arrive just in time to bear the full force of its anger.

The roar of the triceratops and screeches of the velociraptors tell you that a battle has broken out behind you, but you don't wait around to see the result!

Go to 5.

29

You floor the accelerator. The jeep lurches forwards and breaks free of the mud.

The dinosaur gives chase and barges the jeep, using its tail to smash the bodywork.

To shoot the ankylosaurus with your dart gun, go to 45.

To drive faster, go to 41.

30

The drones show that all the dinosaurs are heading back to their underground lair, using the ramp you spotted yesterday.

Duarte points at the rising sun. "It seems they don't like the light."

You nod. "My guess was correct — they'll hide down there until nightfall. If we destroy that ramp, they'll be trapped."

To blow up the ramp at once, go to 17.

To wait until all the dinosaurs are back underground, go to 20.

31

Deciding to act at once, you pack an army jeep with kit including explosive charges to destroy the dinosaurs' route to the surface.

Duarte comes to report. "I have equipped a backup truck," she says, "but it has a fault. It will take hours to fix. You can wait, or my men and I can meet you at dawn tomorrow."

To wait for the backup vehicle, go to 42.

To set off immediately, go to 2.

Feeling the tug of an underwater current, and diving down to follow it, you are swept through a narrow opening. The liopleurodon attacks but you are moving too quickly.

You emerge into an underground lake. In the middle is an island made by rock and earth from the cenote's collapsed roof. Vines and long roots dangle from the forest floor above.

All around the lake, dinosaurs are drinking. The ramp you have to destroy stretches up behind them.

You find a hidden spot and go ashore. Discarding your scuba gear, you try to sneak towards the ramp — but triumphant screeches tell you that you have been spotted by a pack of velociraptors.

To dive back into the lake, go to 18.

To use one of the dinosaurs as cover, go to 48.

To run and hide, go to 4.

33

"The Tyrannosaurus rex is the biggest threat," you tell Duarte. "We'll go after that first."

You give the order to "Move out!" and lead the soldiers into the forest. The drone continues to track the T. rex.

Suddenly, the drone operator's screen goes blank. You look up to see a pterosaur sailing past with the crippled machine in its talons. *Uh-oh*, you think. *Our eye in the sky is toast.*

If the Tyrannosaurus rex realises you're following it and decides to attack, you won't have any warning.

Your instincts prove right.

Moments later, with a roar and a crash of falling trees, the T. rex is upon you. The terrified soldiers fire a few bursts without effect, then drop their weapons and run, leaving you to face the monster alone.

Go to 27.

34

"Tell him to go away," you say.

Duarte looks unhappy. "Many people here are descended from the Maya. Their priests have great power. This one could help us."

A rumble of thunder makes you look out the window. The weather is getting worse.

Duarte's telephone rings. She answers it in Spanish, then turns to give you the news.

"We can do nothing until this storm passes. All flights are grounded."

You shrug. "Okay. If there's nothing else to do, I may as well see this priest."

Go to 6.

35

You decide you don't want to risk meeting a triceratops, and turn aside from the trail.

But before long, you hear the sounds of pursuit again — and this time, there is nowhere to hide from the velociraptors.

As the pack closes in, you take the only possible way out.

Go to 27.

36

You run away from the jeep, but find yourself in the path of a stampeding herd of antarctosaurus.

You stagger and fall beneath their thundering feet. You are about to be trampled into jelly!

Go to 27.

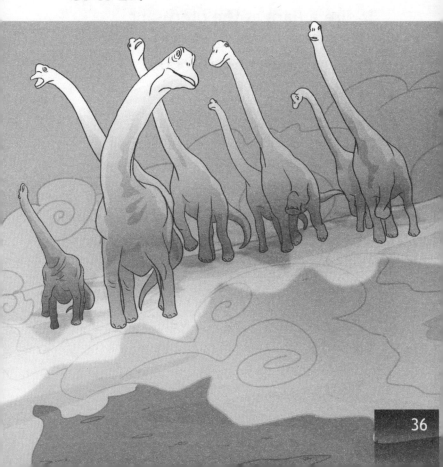

37

You reach for your dart gun and take aim, but the pilot is zigzagging to dodge the pterosaur's attack. Big as your target is, you cannot hit it while you are being flung around the sky.

To order the pilot to try to escape, go to 46.

To fire a flare at the pterosaur, go to 11.

To try to land the helicopter, go to 40.

38

You run quickly to the nearest tree and begin to climb.

But the velociraptors' long, curved claws make them excellent climbers. They chase you up the tree, gaining all the time.

You realise that there is only one way out of this situation.

Go to 27.

39

The winch-man fires a flare that explodes
in the dinosaur's face — but the T. rex just
closes its eyes and jerks its head.

You lose your grip on the ladder and tumble
helplessly into the creature's gaping jaws.
There is only one escape!

Go to 27.

"Land!" you tell the pilot.

He tries to put the helicopter down, but the clearing he chooses is too small. Its rotors are smashed to pieces by surrounding trees. The helicopter crashes to the ground, landing at the feet of a startled stegosaurus. The outraged creature attacks. You are about to be squashed!

Go to 27.

41

You drive faster and outdistance the ankylosaurus. But your jeep is skidding badly from rut to rut, and eventually it bounces off the road and overturns.

You crawl out of the wreckage, unhurt.

To abandon the jeep and continue on foot, go to 24.

To stay put and wait for daylight, go to 7.

42

You decide to wait. Hours later, the camp erupts into chaos. You hear cries, gunshots and explosions. You run outside to see a huge stegosaurus using its tail to smash a helicopter as if it were made of tinfoil.

The dinosaur turns from the helicopter and charges towards you with gaping jaws. You hold the amulet the old priest gave you. If ever you needed the help of Mayan spirits, it's now!

Go to 27.

43

The villagers suddenly start screaming, and run away in panic. You turn, and look up into the powerful jaws of the T. rex.

The high explosive charges you are carrying take time to prepare, and time is something you do not have. Your only usable weapon is your dart gun.

You fire a dart into the T. rex's mouth. Your aim is good, but the tranquiliser dose is far too small to knock out such an enormous creature. The dart has no effect. You have only one option left...

Go to 27.

44

"Throw me a gun!" you yell.

The pilot drops a pistol. You catch it and fire at the T. rex. The bullets just bounce off! The angry beast shakes its head, smashing the helicopter against the cavern rim. It explodes.

You have failed at the last hurdle!

Go to 27.

45

You snatch up your gun and fire a tranquiliser dart at the ankylosaurus. But the dart is designed to go through the soft skin of mammals, not the armoured hide of a dinosaur!

The creature gives a final shove, and the jeep crashes into a tree. The impact knocks the breath from your body. The engine cuts out. You try to restart it, but the motor is dead. You have no choice but to abandon the jeep.

Go to 36.

46

"Get us out of here!" you tell the pilot.

But the pterosaur attacks. Its claws tear the rotors to pieces and the crippled aircraft falls from the sky.

The priest's amulet is the only hope you have!

Go to 27.

47

The situation is bad, but you are an expert at moving stealthily through the jungle and not letting your scent carry to predators. As you creep away, you switch on your radio to call Duarte.

The radio screeches into life. "Hunter, what is your position?"

You realise you must have accidentally turned the receiver up to full volume by mistake. You switch off the radio instantly, but now the velociraptors know you are there.

To run, go to 15.
To hide, go to 26.

48

You spot a triceratops and hide behind it, keeping its great armoured body between you and the velociraptors. The distracted beast doesn't notice you, and the hunters, having lost sight of you, can't pick up your smell.

As soon as the pursuit has gone by, you sprint for the ramp and start putting down explosive charges.

But as you are setting the timer on the last charge, a bellow freezes your blood. The T. rex has spotted you! As it lumbers down the ramp, its roars attract the velociraptors. They join the hunt.

To hide, go to 4.
To make for the pool, go to 18.
To take refuge on the island, go to 8.

49

You call Duarte and give her your location.

"The truck is fixed," she says. "We'll be with you soon. The helicopter is on standby and it can be here in a few minutes."

Soon, the truck bounces into view. Duarte has brought a squad of commandoes, and all the equipment you asked for, including three drones and a set of scuba diving gear.

As the sun rises, you send up the drones. Immediately, one of the operators calls you across. Her drone has located the T. rex.

To track down the T. rex, go to 33.

To find out what the rest of the dinosaurs are doing, go to 30.

50

You fly over the crater. Duarte examines your handiwork with approval.

"The pterosaurs can still get out," she says, "but we will have the opening netted by nightfall."

You mop your brow. "Good. But if you have any more trouble with dinosaurs, do me a favour — call on someone else!"

Duarte laughs. "Sorry, my friend, I would call on you again. You are a real hero!"

I HERO Quiz

Test yourself with this special quiz. It has been designed to see how much you remember about the book you've just read. Can you get all five answers right?

Question 1

Where are you at the beginning of your dinosaur adventure?

A   Mesozoic era

B   Guatemala

C   Colorado, USA

D   Antarctica

Question 2

How are the dinosaurs getting out of
the cenote?

A   a ramp made of earth and rock

B   a ladder

C   a man-made bridge

D   through a swamp

Question 3

What type of dinosaur attacks the helicopter?

A   stegosaurus

B   ankylosaurus

C   pterodactyl

D   velociraptor

Question 4

What does the Mayan priest give you?

A   an amulet decorated with a serpent

B   a gold coin

C   a dart gun

D   his sacred headdress

Question 5

How is the ramp destroyed?

A   gunfire

B   helicopter crushes it

C   dinosaur smashes into it

D   explosive charges

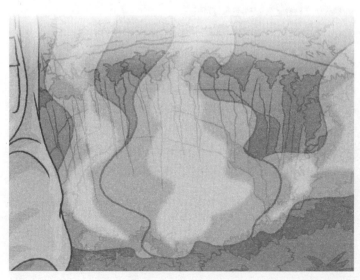

About the 2Steves

"The 2Steves" are one of Britain's most popular writing double acts for young people, specialising in comedy and adventure. They  perform regularly in schools and libraries, and at festivals, taking the power of words and story to audiences of all ages.

Together they have written many books, including the *Monster Hunter* series. Find out what they've been up to at:
www.the2steves.net

About the illustrator: Judit Tondora

Judit Tondora was born in Miskolc, Hungary and now works from her countryside studio. Judit's artwork has appeared in books, comics, posters and on commercial design projects.

To find out more about her work, visit:
www.astound.us/publishing/artists/ judit-tondora

Have you completed these I HERO adventures?

Battle with monsters in Monster Hunter:

ALIEN
978 1 4451 5878 5 pb
978 1 4451 5876 1 ebook

ZOMBIE
978 1 4451 5935 5 pb
978 1 4451 5933 1 ebook

VAMPIRE
978 1 4451 5936 2 pb
978 1 4451 5937 9 ebook

GHOST
978 1 4451 5939 3 pb
978 1 4451 5940 9 ebook

WEREWOLF
978 1 4451 5942 3 pb
978 1 4451 5943 0 ebook

MUTANT
978 1 4451 5945 4 pb
978 1 4451 5946 1 ebook

Defeat all the baddies in Toons:

KILLER CUSTARD
Steve Barlow · Steve Skidmore
978 1 4451 5930 0 pb
978 1 4451 5931 7 ebook

ROBIN HAMSTER
Steve Barlow · Steve Skidmore
978 1 4451 5921 8 pb
978 1 4451 5922 5 ebook

ENTER the PENGUIN
Steve Barlow · Steve Skidmore
978 1 4451 5924 9 pb
978 1 4451 5925 6 ebook

KUNG FU KITTEN
Steve Barlow · Steve Skidmore
978 1 4451 5918 8 pb
978 1 4451 5919 5 ebook

Also by the 2Steves...

Tip can't believe his luck when he mysteriously wins tickets to see his favourite team in the cup final. But there's a surprise in store ...

Big baddie Mr Butt Hedd is in hot pursuit of the space cadets and has tracked them down for Lord Evil. But can Jet, Tip and Boo Hoo find a way to escape in a cunning disguise?

Jet and Tip get a new command from Master Control to intercept some precious cargo. It's time to become space pirates!

The goodies intercept a distress signal and race to the rescue. Then some 8-legged fiends appear ... Tip and Jet realise it's a trap!